"It's about a magical snow dragon," explained Squirt, "with an orange horn."

Sparkie's eyes lit up. "And the Snow Dragon breathes snow instead of fire. It lives in a beautiful ice palace in the woods."

"Books are great," agreed Mike, "but it's a lot more fun outside in the snow."
"Actually," admitted Sparkie, "I've never been out in it."
Mike gasped. The dragons were his knightly helpers. They couldn't just stay in whenever the weather turned chilly!

"By the King's crown, that's it!
I'm Mike the Knight and my mission is to get my dragons used to the snow!"

The bold knight-in-training put on his armour and slid down the secret chute to Galahad's stable. Now he was ready to ride out for a wintry adventure!

Mike drew his enchanted sword.

"A carrot? How am I going to use that to help with my mission?" he wondered.

Suddenly Sparkie skidded into the icy courtyard. **"Woohoo!"** he bellowed. "Snow is fun! I love it!"

Squirt stepped out nervously. A big drift of snow slid off the castle balcony and landed on Squirt.

Poouuuff!

"Ooh!" squealed Squirt. "It's too cold!"

"Come on," grinned Mike. "We're going on a knightly snow trek."

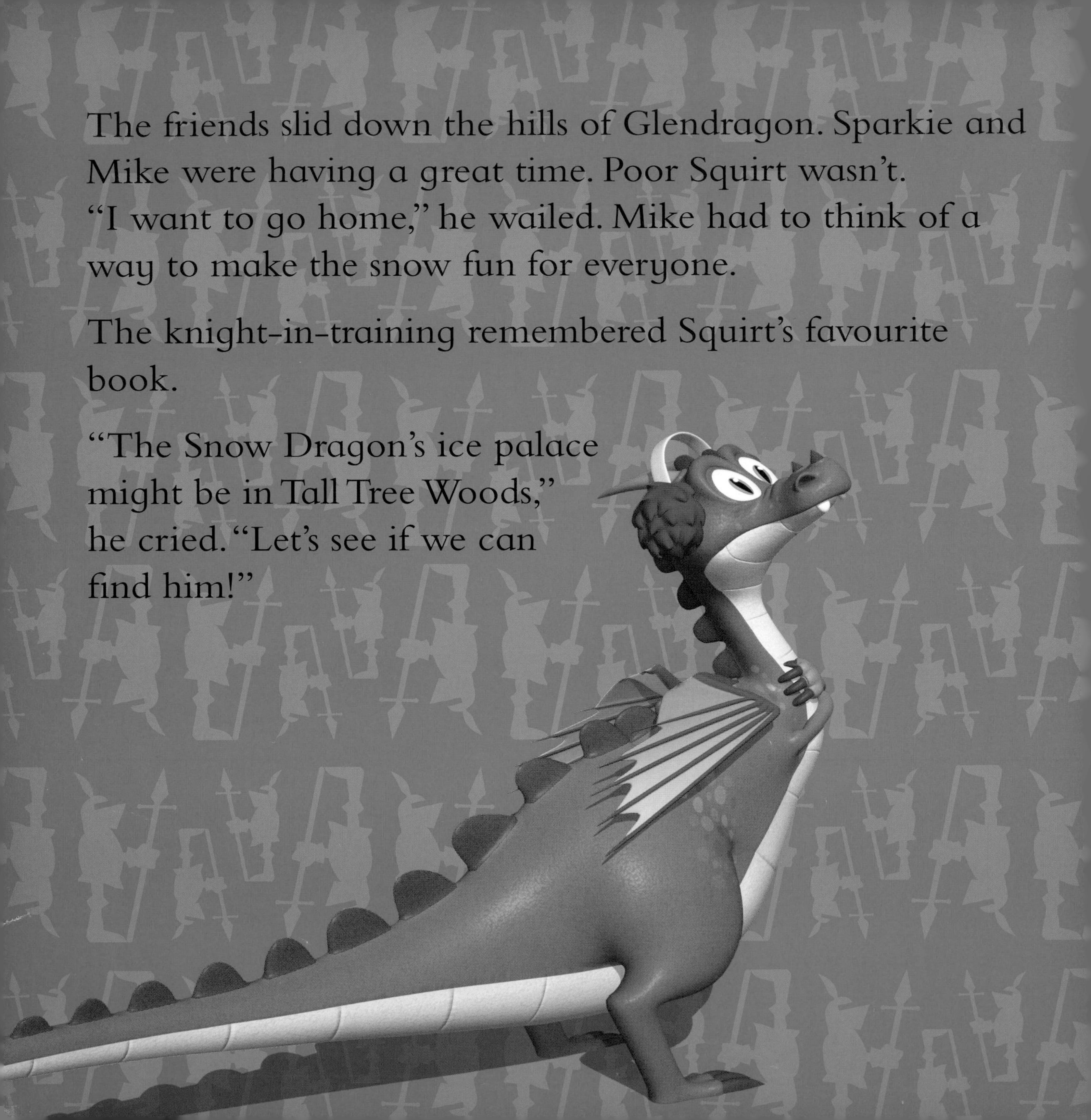

The friends slid down the hills of Glendragon. Sparkie and Mike were having a great time. Poor Squirt wasn't. "I want to go home," he wailed. Mike had to think of a way to make the snow fun for everyone.

The knight-in-training remembered Squirt's favourite book.

"The Snow Dragon's ice palace might be in Tall Tree Woods," he cried. "Let's see if we can find him!"

Mike and his friends trudged through the trees. They'd been walking for ages, but there was no sign of the Snow Dragon! Squirt's teeth chattered with every snowy step.

"The ice palace must be round the next corner," said Mike cheerfully.

Squirt stopped.
"I'm s-s-slipping and w-w-w-et and c-c-c-c-old!"
he shivered. "I'm going home."
Mike pointed to the ground.
"Look!" he shouted. "**Snow Dragon** footprints!"

Squirt perked up. The Snow Dragon had to be close! He couldn't wait to share a warm hot chocolate in the ice palace.

Sparkie took a closer look at the mysterious marks in the snow.

"No, Mike," he frowned. "Those are **my** footprints."

Mike did feel bad for fibbing, but at least he'd managed to cheer up Squirt.

Suddenly a loud yelp echoed through the trees.

"Come on, Galahad!" cried Mike.

"Mike the Knight to the rescue!"

Galahad skidded to a stop at the top of a steep hill. Down at the bottom, Squirt was stuck in a giant snowball. Mike leapt into action. "Hang on!" he shouted, tossing his shield into the air. The plucky knight used the shield to sledge all the way down the hill.

"Squirt!" panted Mike. "Are you OK?"

"No!" sobbed Squirt. "Now I'm r-r-r-really w-wet and very **very** c-c-cold and I didn't find the Snow Dragon!"

It was time for Mike to tell the truth.
"I only said that stuff about the Snow Dragon to stop you going home," he said quietly.

"You m-m-mean he isn't real?" gasped Squirt.
"I'm really sorry," replied Mike.

"I thought I was going to see a Snow Dragon," whispered Squirt. "Now I never will."

Mike didn't like making his friends sad. Suddenly he had a wonderful, wintry idea.

"It's time to be a knight and do it right!" he declared.

Everybody got to work.
First they built up a giant
mound of snow...

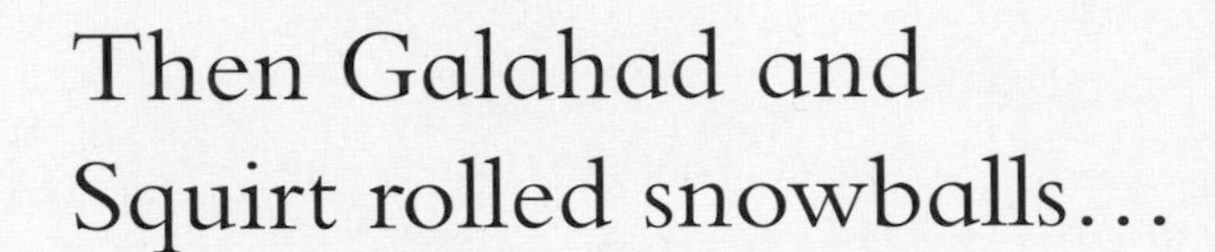

Then Galahad and
Squirt rolled snowballs...

Mike stuck on two stones
for eyes...

...and the Snow
Dragon was ready!

“We just need one more thing,” beamed Mike, pulling out his enchanted sword.
Squirt took the carrot off the end and put it on the Snow Dragon.
“Now he’s got an orange horn on his nose,” Squirt announced proudly.
The Snow Dragon was perfect!

"Hey!" cried Squirt. "I've completely forgotten about being wet and cold!"

Sparkie chuckled. "That's because you've been having fun!"

Mike felt very proud of the dragons. Now they'd be ready for an adventure whenever it snowed.

Just then another flurry of snowflakes began to fall.
"Even I'm feeling a little cold now!" grinned Mike.
"Let's have a snow race," suggested Squirt. "First one back to the castle gets a hot chocolate."
Everyone cheered. It really had been a wonderful winter weather day!

HUZZAH!

MIKE
THE KNIGHT

MIKE THE KNIGHT
How to Be a Knight
A POP-UP BOOK!

MIKE THE KNIGHT
Mike's Missions
As seen on TV

MIKE THE KNIGHT
Meet Mike!
As seen on TV

More magical
Mike the Knight books

www.miketheknight.com
www.simonandschuster.co.uk

MIKE THE KNIGHT
The King's Crown
Sticker Book
As seen on TV
MIKE THE KNIGHT
DARING Doodles and SCARY Stickers
Drawing, colouring and over 75 stickers!

MIKE THE KNIGHT
and the Scary Dragons
As seen on TV

MIKE THE KNIGHT
and the Mighty Shield
As seen on TV

MIKE THE KNIGHT
and the Fluttering Favour
As seen on TV

MIKE THE KNIGHT
and Trollee in Trouble
As seen on TV

MIKE THE KNIGHT
and the Real Sword
As seen on TV

MIKE THE KNIGHT
and the Invisible Monster
As seen on TV

MIKE THE KNIGHT
and the Wizard's Treasure
As seen on TV